SKYFIRE

By FRANK ASCH

Simon and Schuster Books for Young Readers
Published by Simon & Schuster Inc., New York

Simon and Schuster Books for Young Readers
Simon & Schuster Building   Rockefeller Center
1230 Avenue of the Americas
New York, New York 10020

Published by the Simon & Schuster Juvenile Division
SIMON AND SCHUSTER BOOKS FOR YOUNG READERS
is a trademark of Simon & Schuster Inc.
Manufactured in the United States of America

10 9 8 7 6 5 4 3 2 1   10 9 8 7 6 5 4 3 2 1 (Pbk)

Library of Congress Cataloging-in-Publication Data

Asch. Frank. Skyfire / by Frank Asch.
p. cm.
Summary: When he sees a rainbow for the first time, Bear thinks
that the sky is on fire and he is determined to put out the skyfire.
[1. Rainbow—Fiction. 2. Bears—Fiction] I. Title.
PZ7.A778Sk 1988
[E]—dc19   88-3193 CIP AC

0-671-66692-4   0-671-66861-7 (Pbk)

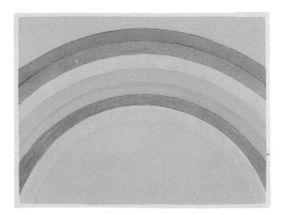

To Fred Levy

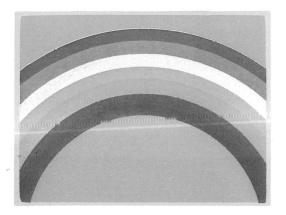
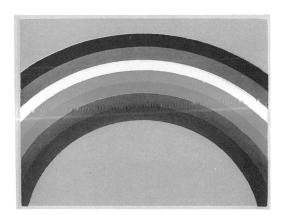

One day Bear looked out his window and saw
a rainbow. He had never seen a rainbow before.
To Bear it looked like the sky was on fire.

"Oh, my goodness!" called Bear to his
friend Little Bird. "Just look at the
sky!"
Little Bird flew over to Bear's window.
"Why, it's a rainbow!" said Little Bird.
"Come on! Let's go find the pot of gold."
"Pot of gold?" said Bear. "What are you
talking about?"
"Don't you know?" replied Little Bird.
"They say there's a pot of gold at the
end of the rainbow."

"What nonsense!" said Bear. "The sky is
on fire and all you can talk about is gold!"
And he picked up an empty honey pot
and ran outside.

At the pond Bear filled the pot with water.

Then he ran toward the rainbow.

He ran and he ran and he ran.

"Look, Bear," said Little Bird,

"the rainbow ends right by that hollow tree."

But Bear wasn't listening.
He was busy climbing a hill.
When he got to the top,
he threw the water at the rainbow.

Just then the rainbow faded away.

Little Bird chirped,
"Look, Bear, I found the gold."

Bear went to the tree.

Inside he found lots of *golden* honey.

He filled his pot...

...and took it home.

That night Little Bird came over.

Bear made honey cakes.

After dinner they went for a boat ride.

For a long while they were very quiet.

Then Little Bird said, "So it *was* a
rainbow, and I found the pot of gold!"

"Oh, no, it wasn't," replied Bear.
"It was a sky fire...